CAUGHT LOOKING
BY THE ROOMMATE

Straight to Gay First Time Story

Michael Levi

ISBN: 9798423012762
Imprint: Independently published

1st edition

Cover design by: Michael Levi

CONTENTS

CHAPTER 1

I groaned, finding it impossible to sleep right now. Midterms, finals, parties, and all that jazz. College life just couldn't get any better, could it? It could, actually. I just didn't think that it would ever. Something was missing in it and that was having sex. All the time. Every night. Every time I was horny.

Time was passing and I couldn't stop tossing and turning on the bed. I opened my eyes as I found the rotating blades of the ceiling fan. Round and round they went as though it was teasing me. *What the hell do you think you're doing? You're wasting your time lying in your bed right now. Get out of it now!* I could almost hear it saying that to me.

I was about to adjust the pillow when my phone buzzed all of a sudden. Just like everyone my age, I fished my phone off the nightstand and turned on the screen. I didn't think that I was going to find anything interesting on it, but the icon piqued my interest. Someone had sent me a private message and I knew that meant that it was something I needed to check out right now.

At least something was going to break the monotony of my night. And if I was in luck, maybe it would even get my mind off the nagging thoughts swirling in my mind. They were like flies pestering me all the time.

I pressed on the icon, the message loading. The first thing I noticed was that the message wasn't from one of my friends, but from a guy I couldn't care less about. He was despicable, always thinking so highly of himself all the time, and showing off his muscles.

Well, he had every right to show them off. He was a beast of nature. Not too big, but massive enough to make me jealous of him. I wouldn't say that I wasn't someone that didn't work out, but I wasn't anything like him. I was leaner, more compact and, in a fight, I wouldn't stand a chance against him.

The image finished loading and... Oh my God.

I couldn't believe what I was seeing. The photo was indeed sent by my roommate and it showed his... junk. It was jaw-dropping. Given the size of his hand – something that I was used to, since we shook hands often – I'd say that his dick was a solid 10-inches in length, which was something I never thought possible. I never thought that someone could have a dick so big, so thick, and veiny...

And I didn't even know why I was still checking it out. Alright, he was big – much bigger than I was – thick, veiny, jaw-dropping, and all those things, and his balls were just as heavy-looking as the rest, but I still shouldn't be checking out his junk as if...

As if I was thinking about sucking it off or doing something similar. First, I was straight as an arrow. I didn't date girls, but when I was watching porn, I imagined that I was the guy and the woman was moaning my name. I never even paid any attention to the actors themselves, just the actresses, who were always hot and jaw-dropping. Just thinking about them right now was making my shaft a little hard.

Well, I couldn't sleep before and now it was too late for that, I thought. I wasn't going to be able to sleep with my mind going back and forth over what I'd seen. He'd obviously sent that nude to someone else and soon he'd realize that he'd sent it to me.

Brock would look at me weirdly and would stop being my friend. We didn't do many things together, but I was comfortable with how things were. We treated each other fairly, he didn't try dipping his toes in my life and be too nosey, and I didn't bother trying to find out what was going on in his life.

He didn't have a girlfriend, I remembered. He probably was sexting with one of his dates and sent the nude by accident.

I turned off the screen of the phone, realizing that there was no point in continuing to look at the photo. But when the screen wasn't showing anything anymore, I found it difficult not to think about his nude. There was something that kept drawing me back to it, and I didn't know what it was.

I pondered deleting the photo on my device, sending him a quirky short message saying that he sent it to the wrong person and that everything was fine, but then I realized that I didn't want to do either of those things.

I was going to say to Brock that I deleted the photo and was going to pretend I didn't see anything, but that was about it. I couldn't delete the photo for... posteriority reasons. What if he ever decided to hurt me one day? I couldn't let such a thing happen without having something that I could use against him.

Nevertheless, the true reason why I didn't want to delete his photo on my phone was that I wanted to look at it again as many times as possible.

Me: Hey, Brock, you sent the nude to the wrong person hahahahaha. It's okay, though. I just finished deleting it.

Brock: Bro, I'm so fucking drunk right now I don't even know what I'm doing anymore. Fuck. I thought I'd sent it to Amelie. I'm such an idiot. Thanks for telling me that you deleted it, though.

So that was that and now I had his photo stored on my phone. I could check it out again as many times as I wanted, which was better than looking up porn photos online. There was something 'different' about the nude of a person I knew personally that aroused me to levels I never thought reachable.

I turned on the screen of the phone again and spent what were minutes checking out the nude, dissecting every detail of it. The way he was gripping his shaft, pressing his hand against his low-hanging balls, that his scrotum was shaved, and pretty much everything else that my eyes could delight themselves on were making me drool.

I couldn't believe that a straight guy like me was feeling entranced by the nude of another dude, and I was pretty sure that meant that things couldn't end with just that.

And then I did something I thought I never would. I lowered my pants, grabbing my cock. Stroking my hand along it up and down, I started to jack off at the photo on my phone.

There was just something about his nude that was enticing and was making me horny, which were both things I never thought would happen. I never thought I would feel this way about a guy's nude.

My hand still going up and down along my cock, I was feeling as though I was betraying myself. It was much more than that, actually.

But even though that thought was nagging my mind right now, I decided not to focus too much on it. I was in a pool of pleasure where I couldn't think straight. I was obsessed with the photo, realizing that it was the only thing I could think about right now as I felt I was getting closer to my orgasm.

My entire body getting hotter as the seconds ticked by, I knew that this was going to be one of the best climaxes of my life. I picked up speed moments later as I said fuck it. This whole time, I realized that I didn't have many things worth jacking off for.

Gosh, his dick was just so big. It would be very difficult to find someone else that was just as thick and long.

I shut my eyes, put my phone back on the nightstand, and then increased the speed with which I was shooting my hand up and down. If my roommate came back into the room and opened the door, he would find me doing this and it would be very humiliating.

After all, I was sure he was the kind of guy who didn't need to masturbate when he was in the mood. He would always just pull out his phone and invite whatever girl he wanted to come over to our room. Whenever that happened, I would always have to leave the room so that they could have all the privacy they wanted.

My hand still shooting up and down, friction sounds in the room, I moaned out his name when I felt I couldn't hold out any longer. My eruption came, hard and throbbing, shooting out my come all over me and the bedsheets. I was still stroking my meat moments after the last rope of come shot out, and then I opened my eyes as I found the mess that I made.

Realizing that I couldn't leave it the way it was, I got off the bed right away and started to change the bedsheets. It took me a while, but I managed to put different bedsheets on the bed. After wiping the sweat off my forehead, I also went to the bathroom and took a brisk shower.

When I walked out of it, I heard someone walking by the door to the room. My heart froze as I thought it was Brock that was coming back from whatever he was doing outside, but then I realized it wasn't the case.

I was relieved that I had enough time to clean up the mess I made, but it didn't fix a fundamental issue I had with me now. How was I going to explain to myself that I just came while fantasizing about my roommate sexually?

And not only that, but I also admitted to myself that his cock made me horny as fuck.

CHAPTER 2

"Whoa, I'm so sorry," I muttered, realizing that I just made a huge mess and got myself in trouble. I threw the water all over his shirt, staining it. I had a bucket of water that I was taking to my bedroom and I didn't realize that someone was rounding the corner of the hallway. I was so much in a hurry I didn't even see his shadow approaching, which never happened often.

I looked up, finding out that the person whose shirt I just wetted was none other than my roommate. We were in a hallway where we didn't have enough space to move around. I could feel his body pressed up against mine, which was something I never thought would happen.

I never thought I would be this close to my roommate.

I already knew he was taller than me, but being this close to him was making the height difference more perceptible than ever before. I had to tilt my head to find his eyes, which was putting me in a very submissive position. It was something he could take advantage of and I was very sure he was already thinking about it that way.

"You just stained my shirt, bro. Weren't you looking where you were going?" He asked, almost as if he was growling. His voice was thick, which was one of the other reasons why I knew he was the alpha male between the two of us. I would never say that to him when he was around, but there was no denying that the thought was in my mind all the time, even when he wasn't nearby.

"I'm so sorry. I didn't mean to do that. I was just taking the bucket of water to our room."

"Did something happen there?" He asked, taking a step toward me. He was so close to me that I could smell his perfume, and it was strong and showed off the kind of person he was. He was always assured of himself and never doubted his choices.

He wore a shirt that clung to his body, delineating the lines of his muscles. It was a hot day outside and he had been sweating. I could see the wet stain at the top of his shirt, right in the middle of his chest. It kept drawing my eyes to it. If he took one step closer to me, I was pretty sure I would be able to smell his sweat, too.

His eyes were locked with mine and I couldn't divert my eyes to look elsewhere. It was as though Brock was controlling me with his stare alone, which was something I never thought possible. I thought I was more strong-willed.

"It's the toilet. I couldn't flush it anymore and so I was bringing the water to pour it inside of it. Looks like I'm gonna have to go back and fill it with water again, though."

Brock didn't say anything, standing between me and the other wall of the hallway. He was making me feel so small. He was a head taller than me, so much bigger and wider that he could lift me in the air without breaking a sweat.

I couldn't deny the thought that was sprouting up in my mind right now. Brock was my role model, even if he was a bully and wasn't someone I could trust much.

He lifted his arm and pressed his hand against the wall behind me, making me realize that I couldn't move away from him any farther. He had me cornered and wanted to make sure that I knew that. Brock didn't need to try doing that hard, though. I was already aware of what he was doing and that I was in peril.

His shirt clung to his body so tightly that it was as though it was almost going to be shredded. I could see his muscles shifting and moving, flexing even. His neck was thick, inviting me to touch it. His abs were defined, moving as he breathed.

Wearing a common pair of jeans, he made it look much more than it was. There was something about it that made me want to buy the same model, even though I was pretty sure that it wasn't anything much different from the model I was wearing.

"Uhhh… Brock?" I tried to call out, but he was lowering his head and was making me think that he was going to kiss me, which was stupid. He wasn't going to do that. Not only was he the kind of guy that would never do something like that, but I was also pretty sure that he was only getting this close to me because he had another plan in his mind, and I didn't think that it was anything I wanted to know about.

His lips were so close to me I thought that he was going to kiss me. I was sweating coldly and I didn't know what was happening anymore, just that this was getting out of control.

But then he picked up the bucket, saying, "That's okay. I'm going to help you fill it up. Don't think that you should be trusted with it again, anyway."

I blinked twice, not understanding where this was going anymore. Brock stepped away from me, going to where the sink and the kitchen were. When he noticed that I was fixed in my position and wasn't moving, he stopped walking and turned to look at me.

"You coming or what?" He asked, ripping me out of my reverie. I didn't have any time to lose, so I went there with him, my mind still going back and forth over what happened. And what did happen, anyway? He was on the verge of kissing me, as though he was sniffing my smell, and then he just stopped and was now going to help me.

I was behind him in the kitchen, dissecting his backside with my eyes. His back was extremely wide and sturdy. I didn't want to admit this to myself, but I wondered what I would feel like if I were to rest my head on his backside.

I was just so horny right now and lonely. I needed to do something about that. I needed a girlfriend and I was sure I wasn't going to get one anytime soon. It was just so difficult getting their attention nowadays.

Brock was in front of the sink, turning on the faucet as he put the bucket below it. He was filling it with water, doing exactly what he said he was going to do. He was helping me, which showed me he wasn't pissed off that I wetted his shirt.

My eyes went down, finding his ass. He had his body slightly bent over the sink, which in turn was lifting his ass. It wasn't a big ass, but it was sexy. I could tell that even through the thick pair of jeans that he wore. It was one of the reasons why so many classmates drooled over him. It was one of the reasons why I would never be as successful as he was when it came to sex.

Even if I started to work out and take it seriously, I would never get to his level. I would never have the same ass, I reminded myself.

I didn't want to admit it, but checking his ass out was making me have an erection in my pants, which should be making me question myself about what the hell was even going on with me.

Brock was saying things, as was I. We were chatting as he filled the bucket with water, but our words were coming through one ear and leaving through the other. I couldn't pay attention to what he was saying, my mind focused on his perfect ass.

Even if I was into him, I was pretty sure that he would be the one on top, I reminded myself, which was... actually arousing. After all, I was tiny and submissive even when Brock wasn't doing anything special.

I heard him turning off the faucet, pulling up the bucket before going out of the kitchen with me. I followed him on his heels and was happy that our encounter was ending, even though it was awkward.

Thinking that, I took the bucket off his hands and said, "Thanks for the help, dude, but I'm going to take things up from here."

CHAPTER 3

Walking back into our room after that day where he helped me with the bucket of water, I froze up when I noticed that Brock was in it. He spent so many days far away from here that I didn't think he would be back so soon.

And he was doing something I didn't think he ever would. It was destroying everything that I knew about us and I couldn't do anything about it.

Not to mention that I found it a little hot, too. Even my dick was giving little twitches under my pants. It was one more thing about me that was betraying my true self. I shouldn't be finding this hot, even though it was just so.

Brock was on his bed with my phone in his hand. He was holding it in front of his face, thumbing the screen. The first thought that popped up in my mind was that I should run up to him and snatch the phone off his hand, but I knew I couldn't do that.

For one, he wouldn't allow me. He would just shove me away from him and keep the phone for himself. And there was another reason why I shouldn't even be considering that.

I was pretty sure that Brock was seeing his nude. I told him that I'd deleted it, but it had been a lie and now he was finding that out.

"I'm disappointed," he grumbled, looking at me.

"About what?" I asked, stepping toward him. I wasn't going to let Brock control me again like all the other times we were together.

"You lied to me, man," he said, turning the phone and showing the screen to me. He didn't need to do that. The portion of the screen I'd seen before had already told me everything I needed to know.

My body was shaking. The last thing I thought I'd have to deal with today was my roommate finding out that I kept his nude…

"I'm sorry. I thought I deleted it, but I must've been confused. Let me do that right now," I said, going for my phone, but he pushed himself off the bed and put the phone behind him, on the mattress.

"Nah, it's okay, bro, but you should never lie to me again. I don't like it when people do that. You should've told me that you're gay."

"But I'm not!" I shouted, my cheeks going beet-red. I was lying to myself. I wouldn't say that I was gay. After all, I still wanted to get between a woman's thick legs and worship her cunt, even though that would never happen unless I changed something fundamental about myself, which was growing more confident about the type of person I was.

Brock smirked, approaching me. He looked even more threatening than ever before, something I never thought possible.

"You kept my nude even though you said you deleted it. Tell me the real reason why you did that."

I bit my bottom lip, finding it impossible to contain my erection. It was getting bigger and thicker, and I was pretty sure that Brock was going to notice it. When he did, hell would break loose.

I moonwalked away from him, my butt touching against the wall. Brock cornered me again and there was nothing I could do against that. After all, I was pretty sure he was the kind of guy with a very short fuse. He would wipe the floor with me if he needed to.

"I don't have to say anything," I replied through gritted teeth.

"That's disappointing…" He said, his hand going for my crotch before I could even react. He cupped it, applying pressure with it. I snapped my head up, finding his eyes. He was telling me a million things through them and none of them were good.

"Exactly what I thought..." Brock muttered, widening his smile. If I had ever thought he couldn't look any more frightening, now I was realizing that was nothing more than wishful thinking.

His hand was big, making my cock feel so small.

I put my hands on his chest and pushed him away from me, shouting, "What the hell are you doing?"

"Since I first landed my eyes on you, I knew something was different about you. You want me. You've always wanted me and there's no point lying or pretending that it's not anything like that."

He took his hand off my crotch, taking a couple of steps away from me. I thought that he was finally going to say that he was just playing with me, but then his hand went for his belt and he took it off. He dropped it on the floor of our room, widening his dirty smile.

I couldn't believe what he was doing and the plans that he was building up in his mind. He was finally going to show it to me in person and I was so paralyzed right now I couldn't even turn around and flee from the room.

Brock was controlling me just like in all the other times we were together and even though I was kicking myself up for that, it allured me. It was making me hornier than I was, something I never thought possible until now.

Then, Brock lowered his pants, showing me his bulge. I knew it was big, it was different looking at it in person. My eyes couldn't even blink and I just wanted to get on my knees on the floor before opening my mouth for what I was sure was going to happen.

Brock wanted to put my lips around his cock and the thought of doing that was enough to convince me I should.

His hand moving around his bulge, I knew he was teasing me. The dirty smile on his face didn't lie about that, either. His hard-on was showing too and it was even bigger in person than I thought it was. Spotting a stain of his pre-come on the material of his underwear, I licked my lips.

What I was doing was just one more reason to think I was different from the person I thought I was. I mean, my roommate was turning me on, making me have an erection even though I always thought I would lose my virginity to a girl.

Time was passing as if everything was in slow motion.

His eyes locked with mine one more time before he said, "Do you want to see something else? Do you want to see what I'm hiding in here?"

I didn't say anything. It was pointless even nodding to Brock. I was pretty sure he already knew the answer and that this foreplay was only a formality to him.

"I know your answer was going to be that one or, rather, the lack of it," he uttered, his fingers under his pair of boxer briefs and lowering it. He did it slowly, showing me inch by inch of his impressive shaft. Seconds later, his rod came out, jumping up and down as I felt like I was going to have a heart attack.

Seeing his nude was one thing and seeing the real thing in person was another. His dick was bigger in person, veinier, and I could see all the details I missed when all I had was his photo on my phone.

His hand went for his cock, grabbing it. Brock was different. His dick was uncut and it looked… very appetizing. Gosh, why the hell was I even thinking those things when the first thing I should be doing right now was getting up and leaving?

I knew why. I couldn't help but wonder what sucking off a guy for the first time was like, and I was pretty sure that Brock was thinking the same thing. I mean, I was pretty sure that he would never suck me off, but he was planning on making me give him head and I couldn't say no to that.

He took steps toward me, his hand still stroking his shaft gently. Beads of pre-come seeping out of the slit, I couldn't help but wonder what his come tasted like. As someone who had tasted his own semen a couple of times already, I was curious about his sperm. I wanted to know if he was saltier than me. It depended on his diet, I reminded myself.

And I guessed that now was the moment of truth I didn't think I'd been waiting for all this time.

CHAPTER 4

I had to do it. There was no coming back from what I was doing. His dick was right in front of my face and it was enticing me to do so many things with it. My erection was harder than before, betraying my thoughts. His hand going up and down along his cock, he knew exactly what was going on in my mind.

Brock had always known. Had always known that I was... Gay. It was pointless lying to myself. I couldn't keep lying to myself and thinking that I was going to lose my virginity with a woman.

"C'mon, you can have a little taste of it," Brock teased, widening his smile and showing me his perfect teeth. His teeth were one more thing about him I admired. He went to the dentist often and spent a lot of money on making sure that they were pristine.

I licked my lips again, sniffing the smell that was coming from his junk. It was different from mine, more masculine. His musky smell was intoxicating and it was flooding my lungs.

"Are you sure?" I asked, my voice feebler than ever before. I had never felt so submissive and weak at the same time.

He nodded, caressing my chin. It was the confirmation I was looking for and I wasn't going to waste any time. I was curious, aware of everything that was happening in the room and the door was closed. I had all the privacy I needed with him.

"You know... I never knew you were like this," I said and he shrugged.

"There are many things about me you don't know," he replied

and I knew that our conversation ended there.

There was no point in delaying the inevitable. His hand moved around my head, settling behind it. He pushed it down and I closed my eyes moments before my lips wrapped around his mushroom-like cockhead. His bulbous cockhead, and it was so big I thought my mouth would never go back to normal.

I worked on his cockhead with my mouth, applying pressure on it. I wasn't going to deny that I felt a little awkward with doing what I was doing. It was the first time that I was giving another guy head and I had no idea how to go about it. I wasn't even using my hands to do anything. The only thing I was keeping in mind was that I couldn't use my teeth, which was common sense. It would hurt him if I did that.

"There, there. You're a little awkward, but you were doing just fine for an amateur. With more experience, you'll get better at it."

I knew that Brock was telling the truth, but it wasn't doing much in terms of making me feel more confident. If anything, time was passing and I was still feeling the same way about it. Mouthing his cock, I knew I didn't have another chance to impress him.

If I didn't do everything right at this moment, he would never let me do this to him again, which would be disappointing.

And I was scared of putting more of his cock inside my mouth. The reason behind that was a very simple one – his dick was already too big and I knew that if I put more of it in my mouth, I'd start to gag and cry. It could be something we could do another time when I was better used to this, though.

Gosh, thinking those things right now was making me go wild. I never thought I would be having those thoughts and that I'd ever be sucking a guy off. This whole time, I always assured myself that I was straight.

"Yeah, like that. Ohhh. You're doing it so right."

The way he said those things, his voice very slow and sexy was showing me that he wasn't lying about it. I was giving Brock pleasure, much more so than I thought I could. I thought that my inexperience with blowjobs was going to get in the way, but it wasn't.

Moments later, he grabbed my hand and moved it toward his balls. I looked up, wondering what he was going to do. Brock then muttered something and I couldn't make out the words. Having no idea what he said, I had to get creative.

Thinking that, the next thing I did was play with his balls while I continued to suck him off. His balls were heavy and laden with his sperm. Playing with one of them at a time, I felt that he hadn't come in weeks. His balls were just so heavy, making me wonder when was the last time he bust a nut.

His cockhead was already wet and hot. His pre-come leaking out, I was able to taste it. It was everything I thought it was going to be and a lot more. My tongue swirled around his cockhead, focusing on the lower part of it. It was the section where I knew I'd give him much more pleasure.

I also felt very awkward playing with his balls and tugging at his scrotum, time passing as if everything was happening in slow motion. I couldn't wait until I had a lot more experience with gay sex, which I was sure would happen a couple of years from now. We were both freshmen in college, which meant we were going to be living together for a long time.

When I thought I was already getting used to giving him head, he shoved my head down, his dick going further inside my mouth until it hit the back of my throat.

I was surprised and shocked at the same time, finding out that Brock bore no mercy for me.

And I was okay with that.

Getting used to having so much of his penis inside my mouth was different than I thought it was going to be. I felt as though all of his manhood was in there, which wasn't the case. He didn't even shove down half of his meat and he had plans to add more, making me feel equal parts pleasure and pain.

"I've been waiting for this for so long," he muttered as I tried adjusting his rod inside my mouth. I couldn't suck it off properly the way it was happening before and that was okay. He was moaning my name over and over, showing me that he was getting bombarded with the pleasure that I was giving him.

And knowing that, I couldn't help but smile.

Seconds later, I felt his dick erupting inside my mouth. I tried keeping it in there – I really craved tasting and savoring his sperm – but the man had other plans in mind. He pulled it out so fast I didn't see it happening and when I reopened my eyes, I felt his come all over my face, smearing it.

It was warm, but not too hot. I certainly didn't feel like it was burning my skin or anything like that. I felt it welcomed me, that it changed me. My smile was even slightly wider now than it was before.

I dared putting my tongue out, licking up his release with it however I could. Caressing the top of my head, my roommate told me that he approved of what I did, and I couldn't help but feel that I did the right thing. Then, he scooped up some of his own milk and tasted it, making me wonder if he liked it or not.

I was so horny and pleasure was flooding my body so much I couldn't contain it any longer. It happened way more quickly than I could've done anything to stop it. One moment I was savoring his come on my face and the next I was climaxing in my pants, dirtying it alongside my underwear.

What happened today changed me forever and there was nothing I could do about that.

Brock shuffled over to the other side of the room, picking up a roll of paper towel. He tossed it my way and I grabbed it, plucking off some sheets. Using them, I wiped the come off my face, which was a little disappointing. But the reason I was doing that was very simple. I had classes soon and couldn't waste any more time in the room.

Thinking that, I stood up right away and went out of the room with him after taking a hot shower. I felt rejuvenated, knowing that things didn't end there with just that.

Brock would need even more of me.

CHAPTER 5

My friendship with Brock changed and I knew things wouldn't remain the same. That was why I wasn't surprised when it was the middle of the night and I caught his message on my phone, him saying that he was coming to my room.

I was excited, but also a little terrified about it. There was only one thing for him left to do to me – taking my ass' virginity. He was going to plow me hard, break me with his mighty cock, and I was going to come out of that a changed man.

A changed man? Fuck that. I wouldn't even be a man anymore, but actually no more than his plaything. He could use me however he wanted, turning me into his eternal servant.

Standing in front of the body-sized mirror, I couldn't help but giggle in the loneliness of my bedroom. The light was turned off, but I could still see my reflection in the mirror. I was naked except for one thing covering my body. A chastity cage, made of plastic and metal, encasing me in a way I couldn't even think about taking it off.

Just thinking about doing that would be enough to electrify my body slightly, and thus I quickly pushed those thoughts out of my mind. They didn't belong to me. They weren't a part of me anymore and I'd do well to keep that in mind.

The chastity cage had a hole and through it poked out a bunny tail. The latter was connected to a butt plug, which was preparing me for Brock's painful entry. When he was inside of me and I couldn't feel anything other than his thick shaft, I'd be squealing his name over and over.

I could hear his footsteps coming from the hallway and I knew that there was no turning back. That was why I wasn't surprised when I felt his fingers opening the door before it even happened. It creaked open, the huge and menacing man standing behind it.

"I've come here for my prize," he affirmed, his voice so deep it sent goosebumps all over my body. Feeling his melting presence, I couldn't do anything other than to moonwalk away from him.

Brock closed the door slowly and stepped toward me. As he did that, he ordered, "Stay where you are, sissy little bitch. I'm going to violate you and it won't be pretty."

I gulped, halting as he continued his approach. His hand settled on my shoulder, freezing me again. I couldn't even move any of my fingers. The hold the man had on me with his stare alone was nothing short of lust-inducing and I could feel my dick pressing up against my cage. I hated that I couldn't touch myself right now. I wanted to jerk off until I was unloading my come all over my belly and I couldn't even think about that. This had come to a point where I feared that even my thoughts would hurt me, which was true. Independent thoughts could cause pain and I wanted to feel no more of it.

He pointed with his finger toward the bed, uttering, "Sit" and I could do nothing more than obey. It was awkward sitting with my cage still on, but I didn't give that much thought. Rather, I focused on the man standing in front of me, looking as imperious as always.

He got on his knees, looking straight into my eyes. "Do you understand what this means? Do you understand that you'll be mine for the rest of your life?" He asked, his voice even deeper than before, which was something I never thought possible.

I nodded once. There was no point in holding back where my thoughts and feelings lied right now. I knew I shouldn't even be thinking that he thought anything about me that wasn't nothing.

Brock didn't care about me. I doubted there was anyone in his circle of friends that he truly cared about. At the end of the day, he thought of me as nothing more than someone he could use.

"Good. That's the answer I was expecting from you," he said, lowering his head and planting a kiss on my right thigh. His lips were wet and warm, making me want to make it so the kiss would last for all of eternity. But it didn't and he soon pulled his head back, looking into my eyes again. Right now, I was wondering when he would breach me with his cock. My eyes kept glancing down, finding his bulge. I couldn't wait until he was doing unimaginable things with it.

Then, he lowered his head again, planting another kiss on my other thigh. I shivered, urging him to go on. The smile that crept up on his face was telling. He wanted to do that and a lot more and was just waiting for the perfect moment to strike. It was going to happen soon and I couldn't wait anymore.

"I love your legs so much. Your skin is lovingly soft and smooth, unlike what I was used to before meeting you. I'm so happy that you are my bitch now."

He was calling his bitch straight to my face, which was perfect. I couldn't be feeling any hornier.

He put his hands on both sides of my shoulders and made me stand up. "I'm going to take off your chastity cage and then I'll fuck you until you lose your senses. You want that, don't you? You want that and everything I have for you, right?"

There was no point in holding back what my desires were and so I just nodded, inviting him to do what he was planning. Brock then took me to his bed, laid me down on it, and then produced a key. He inserted the key into the lock of the chastity cage, unlocking it.

He took it off me and put it on the bed slowly, making sure that I was watching everything. I nodded, feeling his rough hand on my ass. He was drawing circles with it, studying what was new territory to him. Brock was the kind of man who liked to take his time when he wanted to and now was one of those times.

"You're so perfect you almost make me feel bad that I'm doing this to you," Brock muttered, grabbing the bunny tail and plugging it out. I had just about enough time to comprehend what was happening before it was too late.

His hand dove into his pocket, from which he took a condom. He moved his hand so that it was right in front of my eyes, his smile widening.

Then, he tossed the condom away, making me feel flabbergasted by what was happening. When I was going to open my mouth to ask him about what he was doing, I realized it was too late.

"I'm not going to do this with a condom. I know you're ready."

I didn't fully understand what was happening, closing my eyes when his hand hunted for the bottle of lube, screwing it open. He spread some of the lube on his hand and then started to smear it all over my ass, including my clenching orifice.

Moments later, he lowered his pair of pants and nudged my tiny orifice with his massive cock. It felt even tinier against that mighty thing and that was putting it mildly.

Then, his hands seized my thighs and pulled me ever so slightly closer to him, until he was breaking all the possible barriers that I still had against the man. He slid his shaft all the way in and then kept it lodged up inside of me, touching my prostate.

Moments passed and nothing happened, though I could still feel his dick in there and that it wasn't moving. When I wondered again what was going on in his head, he started to roll his hips, his pace slow in the beginning. Brock was taking his time as usual and I couldn't believe that I was doing this with none other than my roommate.

He had all the attributes to be my Master, something I could envision becoming a permanent part of his life. I wondered if he thought the same way about it.

Brock picked up his pace soon after, pounding in and out of my ass, his balls slapping against it. When he went still, I knew what was going to happen. One rope after the other, he unloaded all of his sperm inside of me, and it went on for about a minute until he pulled out.

When he did, I fell on the floor, panting. I knew that plenty of things still awaited me in my life with him and I couldn't wait until I was experiencing all of them.

The End

Looking for the first four books of the series? Find them below. The next page has a steamy sneak peek too. Go check it out!

1. Caught Looking by the Quarterback

2. Caught Looking by the Basketeer

3. Caught Looking by the Dropout

4. Caught Looking by the Jock

Lastly, leave a review if you liked the book. It always helps me so much!

SNEAK PEEK: CAUGHT LOOKING BY THE QUARTERBACK

Straight to Gay First Time Story (Bicurious Guys - 1)

I was just a college guy, like all the others. I was trying to fit in and look less like an idiot. Why did I have to stumble into the college's football team, though? I didn't know, but things were working out this way. More and more girls were beginning to show interest in me, even if it was only momentary... and I didn't think it was going to lead anywhere.

I sighed, closing the door by my side when I realized someone was there. Not too far from me, taking off his shirt and getting ready to put on his uniform. I supposed it was appreciation more than anything that was making me feel this way about the guy, even though I was 100% straight. Really, I was, and nothing was going to change that.

But nothing could have gotten me ready for what I was seeing. The guy was perfect. He was in his early twenties, so he was a little older than me, huge, with rippling muscles, and a beard still to be made. His hair was jet-black and his eyes the color of emerald. Every time he looked at me, he froze me with his gaze.

I couldn't stop thinking about him, even when he was in his room and wasn't doing anything more than playing on his computer. I wasn't going to say I was gay. I really wasn't, but I couldn't stop admiring him for being everything I wanted to become. Perhaps he could help me with working out at the gym, but then I didn't know if I'd be able to hide my boner… like it was happening now.

Not only I wasn't gay, but I also had to keep reminding myself that I wasn't a virgin, either. Not in the usual, more common sense of the word, at least. I had some experiences where it kind of happened with some girls… And I'd like to keep things at that.

Austin was now taking off his pants too, and I couldn't stop dissecting his perfect legs with my eyes. I couldn't help but imagine what it would be like to slide my hands over his muscles, feeling his hair, the curves that defined his legs, and smelling the scent of his crotch. Why was I thinking about those things of my team's leader?

I didn't know, but I was already feeling desperate and my boner was beginning to show. I came here with a common pair of jeans and it should be enough to keep it hidden. Austin could never find out that I had a huge turn-on for him, or else there would be trouble. This was a small college in the middle of nowhere, in a region known for being pretty homophobic. I didn't want to take the risk and then be forced to transfer to another university. It wasn't going to happen.

I took a deep breath and looked away quickly when he turned slightly. I didn't know if he was looking at me or not. We were in the dresser room and everything was pretty quiet here. Everything was so silent I could almost hear a pin dropping. I was a couple of feet away from Austin and I was pretty sure he wasn't thinking anything odd was happening here. After all, he had no reason to believe I was gay.

I took a deep breath in, looked back where he was, and I realized he was back to putting on his uniform. But he was still taking off his socks this time. He wasn't looking as imperious as before because he was seated now, his back turned to me.

But it wasn't that seeing him that way was making him look any less lust-inducing than he was. Even now, my body was frozen and I hadn't made much progress in terms of putting on my uniform. I needed to do that when my cock wasn't so hard. I should be punching myself that I was feeling those things for the guy that was always so willing to help everyone out, but it was just... impossible to control my feelings.

I heard the door opening and I knew that meant that things here were going to get more complicated. I could hear them talking out loud, cracking jokes, and laughing. It was the rest of the team. They were walking into the dressing room and were going to see that I was stealing glances at the quarterback...

BICURIOUS SERIES AND MORE

GAY FOR BLUE COLLARS

1. Given to the Cop

2. Given to the Miner

3. Given to the Plumber

4. Given to the Firefighter

5. Given to the Mechanic

DIRTY FANTASIES

1. Filling in for the Bride

2. Filling in for the Wife

3. Filling in for the Girlfriend

ABOUT THE AUTHOR

Michael Levi's biggest passion? Writing steamy, romantic stories that leave his readers panting. He's currently focusing on Omegaverse and bicurious stories, but his collection is diverse and there are books for everyone's tastes. If you're looking for straight to gay, first time, BBC, ABDL, and more, you're going to find them on his author page.

He lives to pamper his readers, every kiss means a lot more than what meets the eye, and he loves his Alpha males. Making sure that every gay first time feels different, Michael Levi writes his stories with a cup of coffee by his side. And for inspiration, he always opens a photo of his new crush.